Princess Stay Awake

Written by
Giles Paley-Phillips

Illustrated by
Adriana J. Puglisi

For Amelie, Fabien, Amélie P, Evie, Olivia & Sylvia

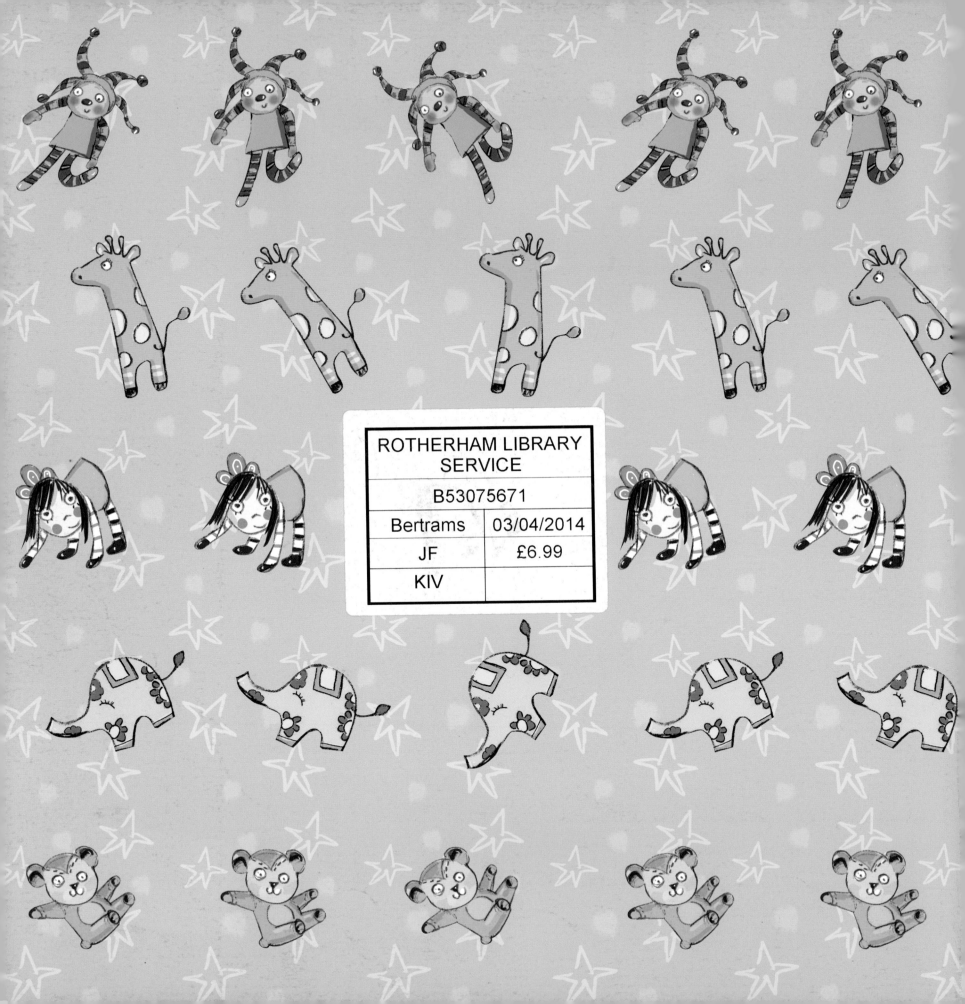

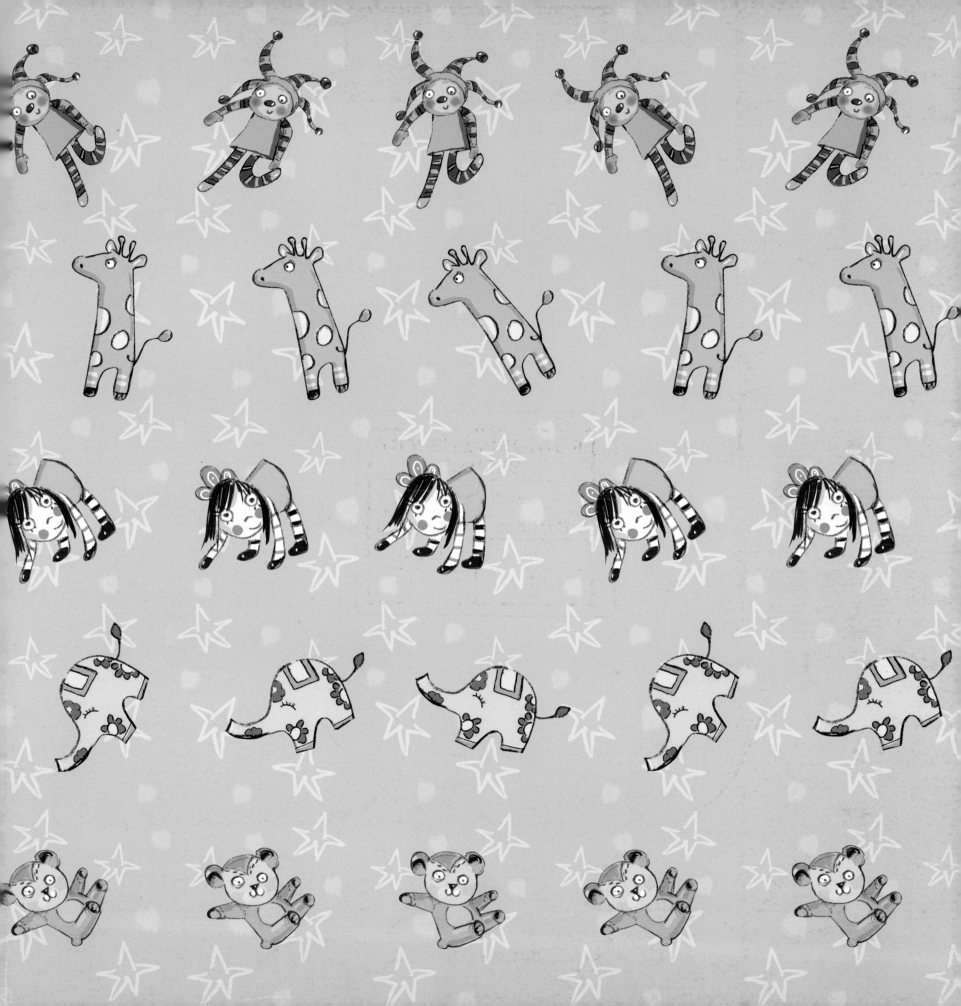

Layla was a princess
who'd never go to bed.
She didn't like to sleep at all,
so stayed awake instead.

She'd skip around her bedroom
and make a lot of noise.
Then, after she was bored with that,
she'd play with all her toys.

The King tried singing lullabies,
the Queen told her a tale,
but everything they tried to do
quite simply seemed to fail.

Layla merely laughed at them
while jumping on her bed.
"I will never go to sleep,"
the cheeky princess said.

The King instructed Wizard Wilf
to cast a sleeping spell.
But when he got the words mixed up,

he fell asleep as well.

They found a clown called Jester Jim,
whose jokes were very boring.

While Layla clapped and laughed out loud,
the King and Queen were snoring!

"What she needs is exercise,"
the Queen cried in despair.
So they called for brave Sir Runsalot
(the fastest knight round there).

Layla had to touch her toes,
then walk and run the maze
but soon the knight was left behind,
worn out and in a daze.

"Perhaps a softer bed, my dear," the King said with a shrug.
So he called the royal bedmakers to make one extra snug.

The brand new bed was not the thing
to help the Princess sleep.
It made her think of a circus
where she could bounce and leap.

The Queen then had one last idea
"I know just who we need!
Send for Grandma right away."
The worn out King agreed.

Grandma came to Layla's room.
"OK my dear," she said.
"I don't think that you should sleep,
please stay awake instead!"

Layla was a bit confused.
She appeared to be unsure.
But Grandma simply smiled at her,
then turned and closed the door.

"I'm Princess Stay Awake!" she said,
giving out a mighty whoop.
But as she cheered and jumped for joy,
her eyes began to droop.

Her arms and legs went floppy.
Her head bobbed up and down.
She then dropped to the carpet
and took off her dressing gown.

With that the Princess gave a yawn and settled down in bed.

All through the palace cheers were heard
(or so some people said).

So wearily the King and Queen
got in their bed to rest.
They slept well feeling grateful
that Grandmas do know best.

The End

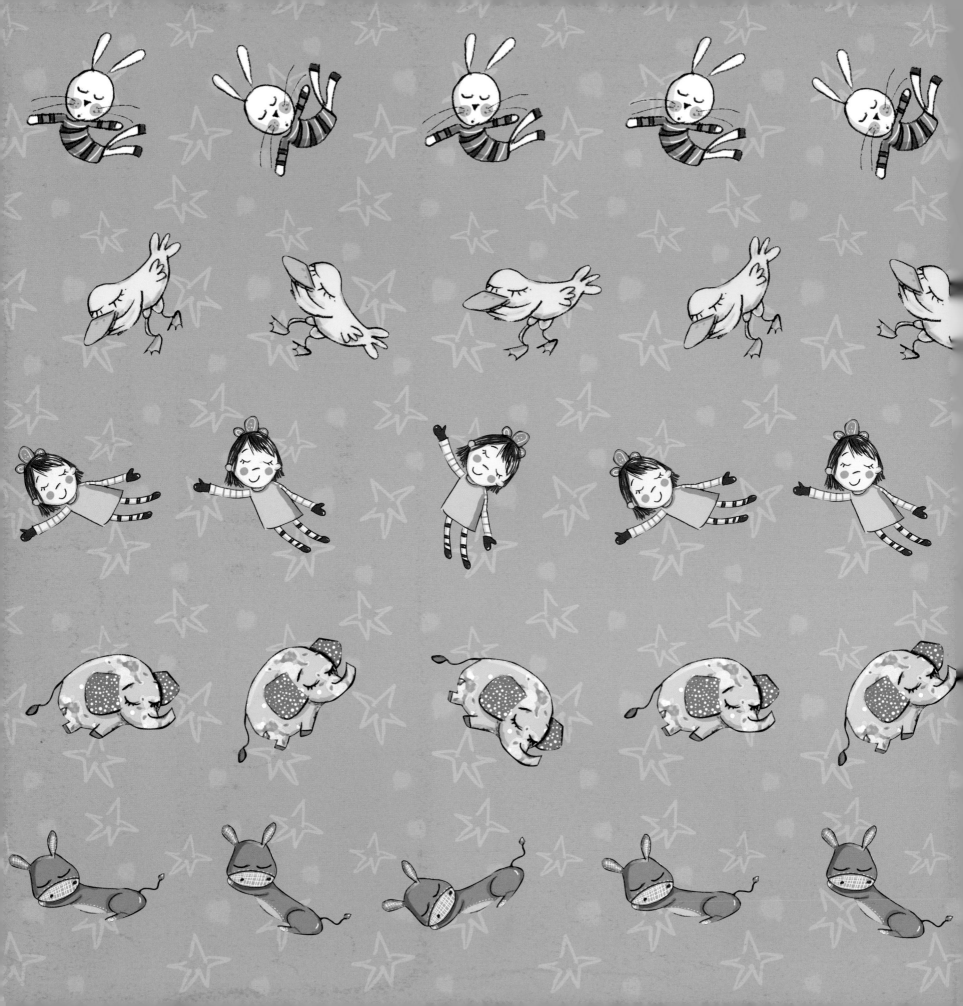

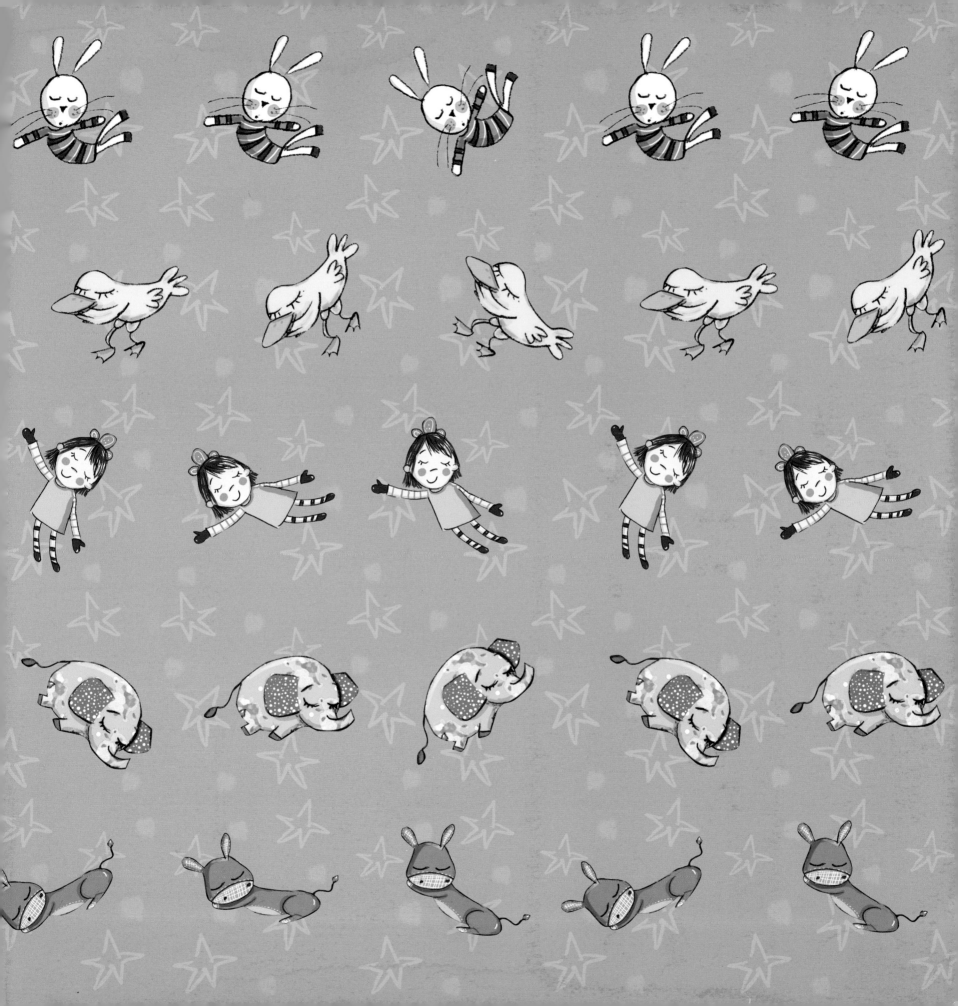

Princess Stay Awake
is an original concept by
Giles Paley-Phillips

Author: Giles Paley-Phillips

Illustrator: Adriana J. Puglisi
Adriana is represented by Plum Pudding
www.plumpuddingillustration.com

A CIP catalogue record for this book is
available from the British Library.

**PUBLISHED BY
MAVERICK ARTS PUBLISHING LTD**

©Maverick Arts Publishing Limited (2014)
Studio 3A
City Business Centre
6 Brighton Road
Horsham
West Sussex
RH13 5BB

+44(0) 1403 256941

ISBN 978-1-84886-109-1

Maverick
arts publishing

www.maverickartspublishing.com